By the Chill Cabinet I Sat Down and Wept

Poems of heartache, recovery, love, light and shade

For my Dad

Part One: Heartache

Life Isn't Black and White – Unless You're a Zebra

That was your fault
This was my blame
You were unkind
I was the same.
You said cruel things
I spat some back
We pulled off rings
The world looked black.
We made it up
With tears and love,
But only till next time:
When push comes to shove.

Endings

Today I put on funeral clothes, drab blacks,
Grubbed for dark socks and t-shirt,
Picked in my heart's wretched debris
For the causes of this death.

There's no corpse to bury or commit to fire,
No rainbow clothes or purple showing honour,
No favoured hymns or poems, no incense drift.
No outward signs of death.

I buy a paper, then make one coffee,
Hurting to lose frying bacon and chatter.
Washing whirls unconcerned, while
Grey rain spatters the silent panes.

I am alone and bereft,
As our dead relationship moulders
In plain sight, but unobserved
By all but those with eyes to see.

Everybody Leaves

My grandma's stroke took her,
A lopsided smile my final blessing.
Another left, an angry case half-closed,
Car revving, then a faint squeal of tyres.

Two of my babies went: tiny, thumb-nail sized –
They couldn't stay long enough to grow.

Lovers have left, they came and went,
Turned away by me, or wanted to leave.

I've left too, closed the garden gate,
Terrified, unburdened, newly burdened.

My mistake was to think that as we were
Good friends, passionate lovers:
You might be the someone who stays.

Cooling Down

It will be different this winter, when frost
glazes pavements and powders roof tiles.
You won't be here to exclaim with me
as we scrape the car, our breathing hazy.

You left after the hottest of summers,
when dew on roses released perfumes
at our open window. Heat rose fast and high,
flooding senses, consuming us as we slumped,
enervated after dawn lovemaking.

We waned, just as the sun receded,
allowing in darker nights, leaf fall and airiness.
Your bags, briskly buckled, crouched a night
in the hall, where our coats once hung.

I felt the first threat of frost in the night air
as you closed my door for the final time.

Neutral Ground

The garden was our happy place.
Anger vanished as we staked up beans,
fed tomatoes in the humid greenhouse, or
forked rich loam into barren spring soil.

Indoors, tempers flared, cups were smashed
and Scrabble boards upturned in tears.

Ending, while suitcases squatted,
awaiting a whistling removal man,
as final gift, I deadheaded roses,
and pulled weeds in the peace zone.

Treachery

Ice slides treacherous underfoot,
a pavement's slick sheen of trickery,
but to be expected, in winter.

Your treachery was a fog of lies:
covering another's body
then eating with your family.

The wind sends out a banshee howl
which can't contest the visceral scrape
from my throat, raw with anger and grief.

Mist curls smoky amongst ancient trees
dampening the leaves, anodyne –
a natural event, soon to pass.

My brain fog, though, clouded the truth,
Allowing all your lies to flourish.

Touch Stones

When the world fractures
though no-one knows but you,
you start by buying a loaf of bread
which forces you to speak
about the weather.

Next, you buy your usual paper
from the newsagent,
which forces you to speak
about the weather.

You can't face more conversation
so you water the plants, carefully,
and do an online order of food you might eat:
chocolate, the cereal you had as a child,
soft fruit which doesn't require effort.

You try to pack the hole in your heart,
cramming bread into your mouth
until the crater starts to fill.

Outside, you buy then write then post
a birthday card to your aunt.
Auto-pilot serves you well.

You phone a friend, cheerfully –
oh, how good you are at faking it!

You sit numbly through a film,
which touches the edge of your brain:
a peripheral light from distant stars.

Then you remember the Faustian pact:

to feel love, to have that soaring arc,
the rainbow of happiness.
Your heart beat down your brain.

You struck a deal with yourself
to be alive again, to feel
rain on your desiccated face.

You had that. Now you have the other:
the pain of loss, gripping your guts
in exquisite, self-imposed, torture.

Detritus

First it was the obvious:
the oddity of stretching out
across two halves of bed,
still buying the cereal they liked,
sudden tears at elevator music.

Then came the discarding, throwing out
the slews of deceitful letters and cards
declaring love, making fake promises.

Worse to purge was the cascade of gifts:
poetry books, hand lotion, perfume,
tiny heart shaped stones, special pens,
Japanese notebooks, a Scrabble set,
imposed clothes, candles, soaps.
all hefted, hurled, passed on, trashed.

This, a hideous replay from a previous life
when a cot, a casserole dish, and a Chinese print
were jettisoned, abandoned.

Burning, raging, I began the purging.
I ended smouldering, as tears doused the fire.

In Other Words

The flurry of love became a trickle, then stopped –
Those bright cards, notes with kisses, poems,
The tender words: love, happy, together, longing –
All ceased.

That daily pilgrimage to the post-box ended.

My Niagara Falls of tears dried to a brittle anger,
I fed the fire with desiccated words.
Bereft of love vocabulary, I turned to bitter writing:
Terse, cold letters to the council, to restaurants.
Always complaining. My language hardened.

Unused words were pulled from rusty tubs.
Blinking in the light, old phrases strode out:
Incompetent paired up with surly,
Slow, pathetic and rude made a dismal trio.
Happy, grateful and thanks slunk into shadow.

On healing, the angry words will return to the tubs.
This time, I'll buy a padlock.

The Kelpies

Huge, blind-eyed, all knowing,
The Kelpies rear up from still water,
steel glittering in the spring sunshine.
One's head is raised, anguished, the other
lowers downwards, sensing movement,
guarding children from water danger.

With a silent neigh, a flick of metal mane,
they search the landscape,
scenting fields, animals, the distant,
pungent oil of Grangemouth, dusty tracks,
and fresh canal water, where boats rock.

Like Tiresias, blind prophet of Thebes,
in the country of the sighted, the Kelpies
have profoundest understanding.
They sensed my heart's sadness, saw
new sorrows and the ancient ones.
They whispered from high in the skies:
"We have seen it all: pain, pleasure, love,
beginnings, endings, fears, agonies, hope.
We have seen too, the joy in the morning."

They whinnied to me, and with wisdom
drawn down through the ages, whispered:
"This too will pass."

Red Rooms

I'm going back down again, reluctant,
into the red rooms, with pulsing walls
to find where the pain is hiding.
I will pull it from its secret place
and stamp on it hard.

But pain surrounds itself so carefully,
with high piles of curling, scented letters
and chunky stacks of memories:
calm walks by peaceful waters,
drowsy, pollen-thick garden hours.

Skulking behind fat tubs set around the walls
– containers abrim with birdsong and sunlight –
pain's sour presence is well protected.
Now, I cannot find and kill my pain
Without first pulling apart
all the guardians of my love.

By The Chill Cabinet I Sat Down and Wept

Afterwards, when it was over,
I had a meltdown in M&S food hall's
dine-in section, so cheery with offers.
My tears splashed: others scurried past.

I've Saturday shopped – over many years,
to nurture significant others –
chosen a main, side and dessert, good wine;
adding breakfast bacon, fresh coffee, bagels.

Other times, I travelled to them: to candles,
bubble baths, kisses, the scent of pasta and garlic,
love in the night and again at dawn,
to the cosiness of chats, the comforts of touch.

With a new wisdom I now recognise
That love isn't always the big stuff,
gifts and all those sighs.
It can just be companionship
and eyes smiling across a table.

Part Two: Recovery and Love

In The Night

Sometimes in the night
when rain sounds sudden and loud
against the glass, or sirens call
from wet, oil slicked streets below,
I wake, and hear you breathe
all quiet through the midnight.
Safe with me. Making me safe.

And quiet, gently, softly
I slide my arm around you,
careful not to wake you
or disturb your dreams
of freedom, birds, sunlight.

Wood Lovers

My lover smells of wood smoke,
of sharp, resiny pine and moist earth,
and of deep loam where mushrooms grow,
where life is formed and leaves decay.
She sheds flakes of brittle bark.

My lover's eyes are smoky blue,
her lower lip a bee sting pout.
I'm wrapped in her branches:
she tugs, gasping, at my deepest roots,
cherishing the greenness of my leaves.

My lover scents the birds, the deer,
the fox's pungent lair, my warm skin.
She braids my hair with daisies,
gathers my sap and stems in her hand,
holding me fast to the mossy trunk.

Autumn will bring a change,
when brittle leaves will cascade,
flurrying along the green blown paths:
a reducing and cooling for winter,
a sinking of the wood, a dying fall.

Then, I will sweep leaves from her path.

Gardening

I watch my lover cutting grass,
that blonde hair falling forward,
shorts and t-shirt dampening.

The mower moves in swathes.

There's peace here, my heart is easy,
hearing bees thrive amongst roses,
glimpsing distant water.

We take the frayed ends of others,
draw them tight and sew up wounds.
Healing kindnesses speak strongest
when delivered with sincere love.

Into the Light

With the passing of days, where weeks
idle down to months, to changing seasons,
there is the moving down the road
forwards towards the blazing beacon.

Fuelled by rising happiness
my feet move onwards, spirits lifting.
Sunshine moves its tendrils round me
warming me back to life, restoring.

A tree root catches now and then,
or a stone needs pulled from shoe:
minor setbacks to progress,
to be expected.

I now walk-joyous, free
past hedgerows, shining waters,
by birds and bees and butterflies,
through cobbled streets filled with
music and laughter and words,
amid the friendship of coffee cups.

Held by and holding your hand
now and always, now and forever
knowing this is now truly forever
I walk steadily, assured,
Into the light.

Wedding Insurance

In John Lewis, amongst the elegant gifts,
lay a leaflet for wedding insurance.

Marriage insurance would be better,
to guard against the cheater, the abuser –
or just to prevent the boredom of rituals,
and that awfulness of snoring.

Oh, save us from 'a nice pot of tea',
– stultifying words from flat cap man –
from cleaning out the shed, and
those same jokes about the mess.

Remove the dreadful dullness of tv,
permanently filled with cricket balls
or awash with football scores.
Spare us the tedium of mechanical sex.

There was no marriage insurance,
No claim against disappointment
and soul shrivelling mundanity.
But, at a cost, there was survival.

Body Map

At 17, I ate chips with brown sauce and impunity.
No extra pounds were gained, I danced them off.

My babies brought joy, a storing up of flesh, heavier breasts,
A settling round the hips and waist, wistful regret
For untrammelled flesh and flat belly.

Two tiny scars, set neat, discreet on my stomach
Show the ending of fertility, and of marriage,
A sad coincidence: borne well, though.

A white scar, star-shaped, fading,
Marks where my wrist broke, tripping on logs.
The wood fed a fire where I sat with my lover
A trade-off, there: pain and delight.

Other breakages, illness and traumas
Seen and covert, have altered my contours.

Sat Nav is clean and clear in direction and choice:
Body maps show wayward journeys
Over crumbling paths and down alleyways.
All journeys end in dust.

Two Mats Away

The people I really wanted
were usually unobtainable.

I had to be fatter, thinner, smarter,
wittier, prettier, less pretty, more stupid
for those who saw me as inferior or superior,
a threat, too small, too different.

So there's been a settling,
a compromising, a lessening of criteria,
a critical look at my own worthiness,
trying to see myself as others do.

There was someone equal,
who ticked all the boxes.
we were happy for a while.

Now, in the Pilates class, I'm stuck
two mats away from the one I want.
Instead, I'm next to a nice woman
who is boring me rigid.

Forget Me Not

She slides the residue from the finished seascape:
oils drift slick onto a new board.
The Iron Grey spume flecked sea
becomes a faint, Misty Grey ghost, ethereal.
The Prussian Blue sky reduces to Baby Blue,
an infant's wide eyes...
Foregrounded fields, narrow furrows of Chestnut Brown
earth
water down to Tortilla Brown trickles.

Her artist's hands, with their paint nails
move the oil traces to create a new work:
a town this time, with Stone Grey chimneys
Caramel Brown doors, Cornflower Blue- jacketed
schoolboys.
The ghost of the seascape haunts its streets.

My last lover's Cardinal Red kiss lives in my skin
Still making my Carmine lips tremble at times.
The ghost kiss, the residue, will stay, but fading
and will slide, gently tingling, onto the blank canvas
Of my next person.

Apple Picking

They glistened brightly, proudly on the shelves
Tempting me. I could almost taste
the crunch of white, firm flesh under scarlet skin.
Oranges, luscious peaches and firm blueberries
sat next to the apples, confident in their appeal.

There was such a person once,
Who dazzled me with such allure
My brain sparked, a flame ignited,
I was consumed with the words
blazing between us. My soul mate.

Then the sparkling skin peeled, warped,
showing the reality underneath.

In the humble corner fruit shop,
carrots spill from dusty sacks,
earthed potatoes tumble in racks.
I choose two dullish apples:
a little marked, a wizened brown leaf
on each stalk: gifts to share with someone
who is exactly what they seem.

Flotsam

The past I had consigned to the sea –
engulfed in grey green lapping waves,
crushed and crumbled under frothing foam:
but it discharged back some flotsam to land,
unasked, into my dreams

Back amongst the wretched debris, my night
self struggled again to be free and clear
to construct, create, heal, forget, forgive.

But still I woke with the bitter aftertaste.

Then suddenly, a bird sang from silver birch
Morning light flared the closed blind.
I turned from restless pillow to see you.

Honest love shone in your eyes
mirroring mine, reaching inwards.

We walked and talked as lovers do
Laughing often, sharing the lovely day.
I flung the night's flotsam into the weir
and watched it dissolve, drown, finish.

Part Three: Light and Shade

Them and Us

The Girl with Red Hair

Isle of Skye, November

Rainbow Balloon

Queensferry Crossing

Each cable was threaded through
eyelets on concrete posts:
a sewing kit for Hyrrokkin the giantess.
She’s in the clouds, using those huge hands
which tugged boats with ease,
to help make our new bridge.

The last heavy wedge is craned upwards,
hauled slow and sure, for hours,
under brittle blue winter skies.

The smiling men, their hard hats sun-glazed
Cheer in all the languages of Scotland,
Where we build bridges, not walls.

Awakenings

In the hot darkness of His Majesty's Theatre, Aberdeen,
we sat, pubescent, some fidgeting, or
rustling boiled sweets from fluffy pockets.
I watched Bassanio and Portia
embrace, kiss so tenderly, enfold, caress...
Strange stirrings bewildered me.

The bus chugged back through darkness.
At Inverurie, we stopped in the town square.
Adults lit cigarettes, some boys went for chips.
The engine thrummed heat, windows steamed
Girls giggled about cod pieces.

Tony, freckled, his mouth odd and eyes afraid,
stood at the bus door, trying to speak,
oblivious as his chips slumped, leaching sauce.

'President Kennedy's been shot. It's on tv.'

A teacher, pale beneath fur hat, ran to watch
the grainy black and white footage,
The silence broken only by hissing fat
as customers stood, turned to stone.

Home safe to the warm, guarded fire,
the old couch, my cat curled on the rag rug:
It must have been a dream, just a tv play.

Then I saw my mother weeping,
and my history teacher dad's face,
looked odd and old, fearful.

Dancing to Glenn Miller

In the cosy room they face each other
mirroring the Wally Dugs atop the mantle.
A sepia wedding photograph sits gilt framed,
clothing coupon outfits on display.
That day, they cut a cardboard topped sponge
and poured small sherries for the ladies.

Cold water digs, soup lasting a week, then better days
of children, train sets, dolls prams in the hall,
good china, a fancy loft extension,
golf clubs, spa jaunts, hard-backed books.
Leaking tents gave way to sunny hotels, good wine,
a gold bracelet, grandchildren, lunches out.

In their bungalow with walk-in shower
and handy pull cords for the warden,
The scratchy vinyl sounds Chattanooga Choo Choo.

Needle jumping, the lost Glenn Miller falters and returns.
Slow as time, they rise as one, smiling,
sticks enabled, they resume the dance of youth.

Counting the Cost

January 1948

Steam vapour, extra blankets and damp flannels all fail.
Anxiety grips her guts, she hears the rasping cough.
In her flat, she ekes worn pennies from the cocoa tin
and sends the eldest to fetch the doctor.
She counts out money – from the Christmas fund,
for the shoes not soled, or extra sausages.
The doctor writes a label for the brown bottle.

July 1948

She wisps back damp hair: her child strains to breathe.
Another girl whimpers in a fevered dream.
The coffers are low: it's the rent money this time.

The doctor's brisk ring heralds in a firm tread,
His tobacco-scented tweed fills the dark hall.
Bedside, he listens, soothes, pats tiny damp brows.
She proffers coins, hesitant. He laughs, dons his hat.
"No need, my dear, it's all free now."

Diving Belle

Immaculate in her dignity, she drowses in beige,
jolted from a half-formed dream by a distant car horn.
Her bones grind as weighted years shift on a cushion.

The dream lingers as she plunges into memories
of Portobello pool, where her young body dives
through salinated mist, twisting in a parabola of energy.
The wrinkled surface corrugates, releasing silver coins,
opaque pearls; the girl emerges seal-sleek, exulted,
breasting towards the lapped steps and chrome rail.

A suicide blonde – dyed by her own hand – sits poolside.
On guard, she knits briskly, red lipsticked mouth counting.
Her chair creaks vault-loud as wool speckles, damply.

The girl springs from the weathered board, the move
suddenly clumsy, as she fumbles the swallow dive.
Her head bangs the board, but she surfaces, groggy.

The lifeguard clicks her needles without pausing,
Calls out: "Dinnae dae that, hen, you'll brak' the board!"

The dream empties: the old woman gazes
beyond the blossom flaring from perfect trees,
and smiles at the memory of the young woman
Who once held silver aloft.

Over The Rainbow

Dundee Pride 2019

High in an azure sky, atop a steeple
Serried colours aim for wispy clouds,
Pushing silken fingers heavenwards.

A joyous congregation marches
in harmony, watched by smiling police.
Sunshine bathes the flock, which blends
and melds, rivering city streets.

Suddenly, with mighty, solemn strength,
the church bells sound on high,
celebrating, affirming for all to hear
That Love Is Love.

For Sophie, June 2019

Angel Pie

Heard by chance, my phrase, decades old:
"Where's my angel pie?" he asks
the beautiful baby – smooth-skinned,
with her mother's smiling, generous mouth.
his hands, my eyes, a grandparent's humour.

Scandinavian and Scots genes knit up with
Minnesotan traits, forming her uniqueness.
A citizen of the world, she giggles, grabbing
his nose, rubbing her hands on his prickly face.
A smile flares upwards, lighting his eyes.

A thread of memory, slack since his babyhood,
Tightens, revives the fabric of current time.
Through concealed tears, for a second
I see clearly what happiness looks like.

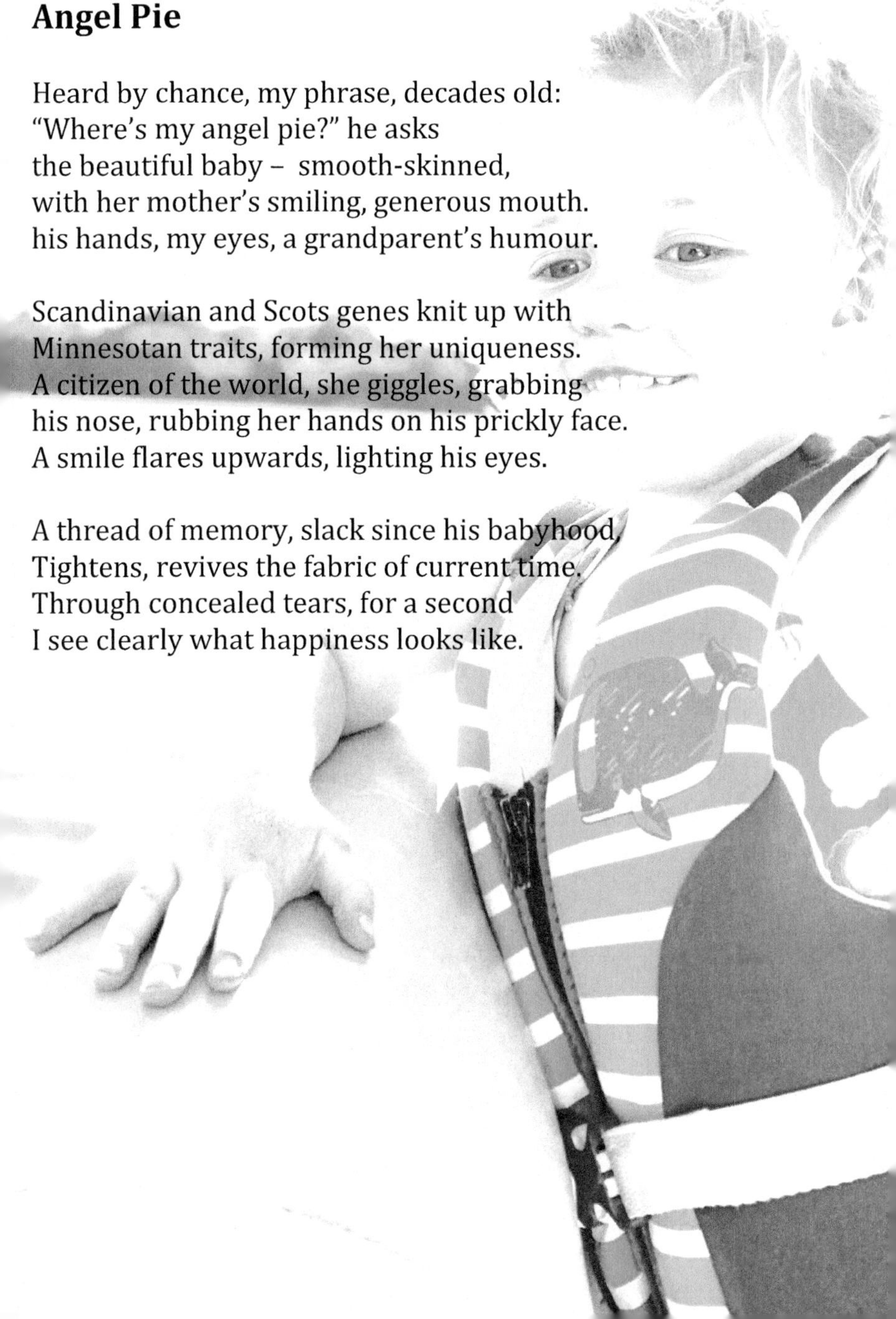

Skye Rose Menzies

Born 23rd November 2014

Skye, island-named beauty, brings blue sky
above smudges of crisp snow.
She parts the clouds.

Still, alert, the infant listens,
Turns to her mother's warmth,
Her father's voice.

This beautiful child is
the sum of both her parents,
and uniquely herself.
She's gloriously new.
Her enigmatic smile engages.

My ancient dream has come to pass.
I saw them, with their baby swaddled,
In a warm and friendly house.

I asked the owls, searched the skies,
Lingered on Iona with a silent plea:
Hoping and wishing.

High, high in the sky
Homewards, over Greenland
I can still feel her warm weighting
Soft in my arms.

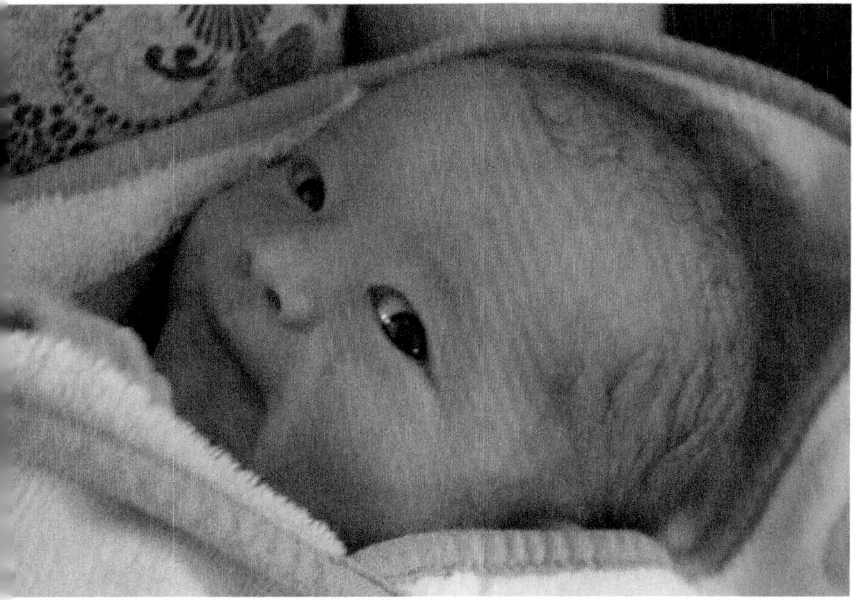

Selkirk, October 2017

A warm returning I had of it,
strolling pavements where once I trod
heavy laden, pram pushing, shopping spilling.
So young, I smiled at my bright-eyed boys,
their blonde hair wisped by Borders breeze.

A kindly returning I had of it,
seeing new landmarks, greeting the familiar.
The trees shed rusty, curled leaves, just as
when boys rushed through them, glorying.

A healing return I had of it.
My eyes, which have seen so much,
sought the serenity of the folded hills,
unchanging in their ancient certainties.
A sudden, releasing lightness suffused me.

A happy returning I had of it,
where dear friends showed that time apart
is of no significance to what matters,
where laughter and memories came easily
and grown children echoed in the new.

Minnesota Daze

Early morning, the sun barely fingering the shingles,
dew speckled the grass, diamonds on green velvet,
dampening the concrete stoop.

Coffee aroma furled upwards in a smoky plume,
the welcome bitterness wakening my throat.
The clean newness of the day was perfect.

The hinds appeared unheralded, a matching pair,
walking sure-footed, fringing the sidewalk, nostrils
flaring, capturing the scents of early breeze.

Their felt ears were folded back flat.
Wary against the ways of men, their
brown flanks quivered on delicate legs.
Just as fast, with joyful bounding,
they vanished, into the woods.
Then birds began to sing.

Wind Power

Hurtling round the houses, the cowsheds,
battering past, along and through the fields,
down lanes, skimming dust from stacked bales
ruffling up the animals' fur,
sliding in under loose window panes,
I slither down green blown mossy ways
up and over and down dales
into the village, hurling scraps around
amongst, between the alleyways,
lifting swirling dropping down dancing
I hurl around the detritus of the street.
I creak the shop signs, rattle the bus shelter
picking up feathers, papers, twigs, leaves
setting them down again
dropping slow, fading, falling
falling, ceasing, at rest.

Rite of Passage

In halls alive with bustle, parents lug cases,
Examine rooms, trundle the corridors.
Students walk the passages from home.
Aglow with clean hair and new shoes,
they swarm, bright-eyed, busy with keys.

My smile set as he hung up clothes.
He saw my face, took off his gold chain
and clasped it round my neck.
'Tug it and I'll know', he smiled.

I mustered a hug, wiped tears of pride,
then left the bright, white corridor, stepping out
into the new life of semi-detachment.

International Women's Day 2022

Woman in the Park

I sat silent on a park bench,
The high hedge shielding me.
The sun begin to set, red fingers
pushing the laden clouds apart.
Across the grass, a distant walker
moved, wrapped against the dusk.

The sound was faint at first, a whisper,
but then I heard the low, keening cry.
I looked, unobserved, and saw her:
An old woman, rocking on a bench,
hunched over herself, weeping.
'I'm nothing now. I'm no-one, worthless.
I'm lonely, hurt. Where's my family?'

Her pain was primeval, wrenched from old depths.
In her, I heard the echoes of all crying women:
The lonely, hurt, lost, abused, overlooked,
the depressed, oppressed, suppressed, dispossessed
Whose voices were shut down, thoughts dismissed.
She cried for those flattered, then flattened.

Small rain began, falling on tangled flowers.
Sitting still, silent, I heard her bench creak
as she rose and wandered away.
Tears thickened my throat, I too wept.

The park's lamps flared, heralding nightfall,
Round, high beacons atop solid iron posts.
The lights split the darkness. I thought
of women who succeed, flourish,

are happy, confident, kind, caring, and whole,
whose tears are dried by others,
who find and give support, who thrive.

I thought of those girls emerging, my own
genes carried forward into the future.

I rose to leave, solitary, yet not alone.
A night bird sang, the lamps shone
To light my way onwards.

Moira's Flannel

Moira in Bearsden picks towels in her guest bathroom,
Layering them into bags, cushioning piles of soap, razors, and shampoos.
In Stirling, Kirsty rakes cupboards, finds tinned tomatoes, soup, pasta.

From crofts, tenements, council schemes, glass and steel apartments, a corner shop in Troon, Morningside bungalows, Aberdeen lunch clubs, a youth group in Hawick, Dundee office blocks, pours a torrent of compassion.

Vans pile high with nappies, pants, trainers, phones, food, blankets.
Westminster, sheepish, joins in.

In the holding camp, beneath unforgiving winter skies,
Ahmed the lawyer opens Kirsty's pasta,
Adds it to the pan of boiling water on his stove,
Opens the tomato tin with newly-calloused hands.

He remembers olive trees, sunny mornings, coffee on the terrace, the cool shade of his office, the faint clicking of computers, dusty games of football with his boys.

His quiet children smile as hot food scents the air.
He wipes their hands with Moira's flannel
Breathing in the faintest hint of spring.

Abbot House, Dunfermline

Tam heard it in daylight hours:
Feet away, people chatted in sunshine,
Stopping on the worn cobbles.

Whistling, he worked on a board,
Replaced many times since the Great Fire,
But once more loose with age.

It was just faint creak at first,
Subtle, a whisper. Then he brisked
to sounds trickling through the ether.

An ancient monk trailed the hem
of his drab brown gown, swishing past,
His tonsured head glinting faintly.

Tam, a practical man, pauses his toils,
overwhelmed by cooking smells:
A tartness of spices, a bounty of herbs
flavouring stews asimmer above a fire.

A serving maid rushes past.
Tam concentrates on cutting.
The ghosts retreat to the thick walls,
To return another day.

Amsterdam

Sickly smoke hangs in the air, across slick canal waters.
Red curtains at windows screen dimly-lit women
Coining to keep children or pay for drugs.
One lights a cigarette, eyes the crowds with detachment.
There's a strange honesty here: just fair trade
Of lust for cash. Euro notes crackle faintly.

Grand buildings sit aloof, resplendent in gold leaf.
They've watched it all over centuries. There's nothing new.
Thousands of bicycles bristle, wheels squeak, crammed, with
padlocks clashing. In serried rows, they squat, waiting.

Small rain falls on tangled tulips; coffee odours contest the dope.
Men on stag trips eat chips, and laugh, nervously,
Eyeing those red curtains.

Left Behind

A small victory, this remaining.

Doris downstairs watches, rolling a thoughtful mint
around her dry old mouth.
Her triumphant outliving assuages, for a moment,
the chronic thrum of loneliness.

Life has ended for me with tattooed youths
carelessly flinging my treasures
into a large, dirty van.
They stub out cigarettes beneath the agent's board.
Whistling, they heft:
the sofa, the walnut desk ,17 cartons of books, the beds,
three boxes of china, my old writing bureau, grandma's
silver spoons in a velvet-lined box, so many pictures, all
bubble wrapped, old letters, scrap books and bags of
clothes
All up high into the van's maw.

They stop, briefly, for a flask of tea, a sausage roll
and a glance at The Sun.

Doris's good black cashmere coat – a little dated –
hangs ready, awaits her taxi ride to the church.
Now I am dead, she has one less person to judge.
She watches still, granite-etched, unmoved,
silent as the chapel echoes with sobbing.

Next, a clink of companionable teacups beckon:
There is cake and company at the Co-op restaurant.

A small victory, this remaining.

Treading the Cobbles

Wind-furled waters reflect glass and steel flats
glittering atop scaffolding as brisk builders work,
adding to the futuristic media city, where
tickertape news flashes are writ large in red
no ghosts of compositors or hot metal here.

Then suddenly, across the canal, there it is...
The Coronation Street set... mossy cobbles,
mellowed brick frontages, doors and hallways,
The Kabin, Roy's Rolls, the hair salon, cheek by jowl
Surprisingly close, somehow, and silent of actors.
There is life, though, a chatter of tourists, mostly women
white-haired, immaculate in beige, with embedded wedding rings
and carefully draped, tasteful scarves.

Outside Sally's house or The Rovers, they exclaim, remembering
Ena Sharples, a young Ken Barlow, Minnie's cat on grey roof tiles.
Prompting memories of their past lives:
twin tubs and soft, white nappies on a washing line.

A young guide, armed with knowledge and cheerfulness
Recites the stories, smiles, clicks cameras to capture the visit.
Life's only certainties: death, taxes and Coronation Street.

Maps

Maps confuse in their certainties –
flat swathes with red ribbons
yellow threads of roads.
There are crosses, rivulets
blue stretches of sea, narrow streams.

Maps are indifferent to their disconcertion
of the traveller, who is thunderstruck by crags,
awed by fierce rocks checked by metal netting,
alarmed by foam bursting over sea walls,
amazed by glittering towers atop city cobbles.

Maps don't describe the air aswarm with starlings
hot with summer tar, bold with festive music,
bitter with winter deaths.

Bland in their information,
Maps only give factual pointers
for how we may travel in life, showing
no cul-de-sacs and no wrong turnings.

The Great Plague of London 1666

The rats brought it, their fleas
carried plague on sea journeys
alighting at the docks, spreading
amongst unwary Londoners.

Silent, the plague swept through city streets,
Trailing death and fear, slipping into homes,
Attacking unwary bodies, swelling lymph nodes
Till overcome with vomiting, coughing up blood
Beset by hideous cramps, lungs drowned:
Death visited serf or lord
Indiscriminate in its cull, spreading outwards.

The red cross of death on doors
Marked the midnight transfers:
Corpses bundled onto carts
Trundled to plague pits.

Then came the cleansing fire, sweeping city-wide
Racing from the baker's in Pudding Lane
Burning, burning through streets, sky afire
Wooden beams and rafters splintered
The sick died, so did the rats and fleas.

Londoners counted the death: a quarter gone
Hastily buried, long-mourned.
A weary populace emerged, blinking
Whey faced amidst blackened beams.

Spanish 'Flu 1918

Battered by war, weary, hungry, lost
A vulnerable world is prey to the unseen
H1N1, a 'flu virus, how bad could it be?
Mutated, it latched onto returning troops
Carrying it home, unawares, to kill loved ones.
A third of the world caught it, in four crashing waves.
Fifty million died.

Covid 19 Pandemic 2020

There is no Great Fire to burn and cleanse
To destroy and heal, to halt the deaths,
To give succour to the dying and their carers.
Instead, we have men and women, white-clad
Labouring through long, darkened nights
Using science honed over decades
And finding a protection to halt the virus
And bring us back to a landscape and life
Changed utterly and forever.

Them and Us

A small figure sits alone
Black masked, head bowed,
Widowed, in a sombre pew,
Her strength and stay gone.
Dignified, she toes the line
Follows the rules, leads by example.
We can only guess at her sorrow.

Elsewhere, the detritus of the party
remains. Bottles sneaked in suitcases
lie empty, reminders of jollity, music,
braying laughter, fun with pals.
Meanwhile, the nation sits indoors,
Lonely for contact with family, friends,
But toeing the line. Following the rules.

Them and us.

April 2021

Girl with Red Hair

Edinburgh, summer 2018

Fading sunbeams glaze the city rooftops,
a final glint and glance on buildings
as the city tries to settle for sleep.

A window flares fiery in the fading light,
Pane tilted to catch any breath of humid air.
Tenements leach out hot puffs of masonry.

A girl drapes on the window sill,
enervated and listless, her auburn hair
ringletting damp in the sickly night air.

Within, blue smoke curls from her lover's cigarette,
mirroring the drains miasma in the weary gutters.

In the nearby pub, the last of the drinkers
throw beer down still-parched gullets,
complaining of the abnormal heat

They've all forgotten about last winter…

Isle of Skye, November

The giantess looks down,
Her crown clouded in brittle blue sky
Her feet crisp with brown bracken.

Mist wisps a chiffon scarf around her throat:
A solitary sheep a brooch on her mossy bosom.
Her skirts corrugate down to a ruffled hem
Of thin white water.

Disapproving as a Morningside matron,
She tuts to her craggy neighbour
"Still they come! More tourists!"

Rainbow Balloon

That morning saw a kindly awakening
In the peace of their home
Where love lives.
Outside the air was spring fresh, tinted with frost,
Sun glazed the roof tops, glittered the fields.

Beloved Olly, his eyes round, wondering,
Shouted, 'balloon, balloon,' his beautiful face
Alight with the magic of the moment.
Adored Lola, hair flying like thistledown,
Rushed, her fairy wings askew, to his side.

The huge balloon, with silken rainbow sails
And wicker basket beneath,
Sat on the frost-smeared grass.

Amazed, thrilled, we watched it rise slow,
Slow and sure into the blue pellucid sky
And disappear from sight.

As sure as sure, for certain,
I will remember this magical moment
Until my final day.

Acknowledgements

Thanks are due to my patient and helpful readers: Jennifer Kennedy, Helen Hamilton, Jennifer Gilmour and John Ross who gave their time, invaluable input and insight during the editing process; to Adam Menzies for his patience and crucial technical help; and to all family and friends who consistently support and encourage my writing efforts.

Printed in Great Britain
by Amazon

19858906R00045